P9-DXC-532

GADZOOKS
THE CHRISTMAS GOOSE

Jennifer McGrath Kent
Illustrations by Ivan Murphy

NIMBUS
PUBLISHING

Nimbus Publishing Limited
PO Box 9166, Halifax, NS B3K 5M8
(902) 455-4286 nimbus.ca

Printed and bound in Canada

Design: Heather Bryan

For information on wildlife rehabilitation in New Brunswick, visit the Atlantic Wildlife Institute: http://www.atlanticwildlife.ca/

Library and Archives Canada Cataloguing in Publication
Kent, Jennifer McGrath
Gadzooks : the Christmas goose / written by Jennifer McGrath
Kent ; illustrated by Ivan Murphy.
ISBN 978-1-55109-794-7
1. Canada goose—Juvenile fiction. I. Murphy, Ivan II. Title.

PS8621.E645G34 2010   jC813'.6   C2010-903080-X

The Canada Council | Le Conseil des Arts
for the Arts | du Canada

NOVA SCOTIA
Tourism, Culture and Heritage

We acknowledge the financial support of the Government of Canada through the Book Publishing Industry Development Program (BPIDP) and the Canada Council, and of the Province of Nova Scotia through the Department of Tourism, Culture and Heritage for our publishing activities.

Mixed Sources
Product group from well-managed forests and other controlled sources
www.fsc.org Cert no. SW-COC-000952
© 1996 Forest Stewardship Council

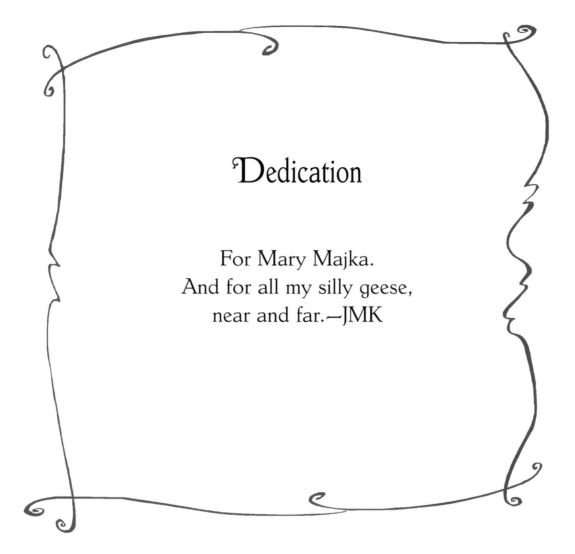

Dedication

For Mary Majka.
And for all my silly geese,
near and far. —JMK

High above Shepody Bay, on a bluff tufted with tamaracks, Corina lived with her grandparents. They lived in a cozy little house snuggled into the hill amid a tangle of wild roses.

It was November. The air was crisp and sharp as a new apple.

Corina was in the yard, picking rosehips with her grandmother. They swung from the tips of the mostly bare branches like bright red Christmas balls.

"Storm's coming," grunted Granddad. "I can feel it in my bones."

Corina stood at the edge of the bluff and squinted in the cold, hard November sun.

The sky billowed before her like a schooner's sail. Down below, the salt marsh spread itself out like a rumpled quilt until it bumped up against the riverbanks.

"Look, Granddad!" Corina called, pointing. A tumble of dark clouds was spilling into the bay. "You were right. A storm *is* coming!"

"Gadzooks," growled her grandfather. "We'd better batten down the hatches." And he went to put the sheep and the cow in the barn.

Corina was in the kitchen making rosehip jelly with her grandmother when the storm struck. It hammered at the door and threw sleet at the windows. It blew the shingles off the henhouse. It tipped over the tool shed and blew the weather vane off the barn.

It blew a Canada goose out of the sky.

Corina found the bird the next morning, tangled in the twisted remains of Gran's clothesline.

"Poor thing!" said Corina. "He can't fly."

Granddad came stomping through the storm-tossed yard.

"Gadzooks," he grumbled. "What a mess!" He stopped when he saw the big, plump bird.

"Hmm," he grunted. "Christmas came early this year." Then he stomped off to rebuild his woodpile.

"What did Granddad mean when he said that Christmas came early this year?" Corina asked her grandmother. "It's not Christmas yet."

"He meant the goose is like a Christmas present," said Gran.

"Oh! I think so too!" said Corina. She stroked the satiny smooth neck. The goose laid its head on her shoulder.

"He *meant* the goose would make a good Christmas *dinner*," said Gran.

"Oh, no!" cried Corina, hugging the bird tightly. "Not THIS goose!"

Corina and her grandmother bandaged the bird's injured wing. They gave him some corn and put him in the henhouse to sleep with the chickens.

They forgot to tell Corina's grandfather.

The next morning when Corina's grandfather went to feed the chickens, an enormous goose exploded out of the door, hissing and honking. Corina's grandfather was so surprised he fell over backwards, right into the mud.

"Gad*zooks*!" Granddad spluttered, shaking an angry fist. "Bird, your goose is *cooked*!"

At suppertime, Corina's grandfather went out to milk the cow.

"Hiss-hiss," went the milk into the pail.

"Hiss-hiss," went the goose in Granddad's ear.

Over went the milking stool. Over went the pail. Over went Granddad.

"Gad*zooks*!" hollered Granddad. "Bird, your goose is *cooked*!"

The next afternoon, Corina's grandfather
was dozing in his favourite chair.

"*Zzz-zzz,*" went Granddad.

Nibble-nibble, went the goose.

"Gad*zooks*!" yelled Granddad. "Bird, your goose is *cooked*!"

High in the chalky sky, an arrow of geese soared southward. Through the window, Corina and the goose watched them go. "Don't be lonely," Corina told the goose. "You can spend Christmas here with us this year. Right, Granddad?" she asked.

Her grandfather didn't hear her. He was too busy reading his book.

101 WAYS TO COOK YOUR GOOSE

The days got shorter. The goose got fatter. Corina's grandfather started humming "Christmas is Coming" under his breath.

The goose was curious about the Christmas tree decorations. He was curious about wrapping paper and ribbon. He was *very* curious about the strings of brightly coloured Christmas lights.

"Gad*zooks*!" howled Granddad. "I'm going to cook that goose myself!"

On Christmas Eve, three very special things happened.

The first special thing was that Corina's grandmother baked her Christmas pies. She baked apple pie, strawberry pie, and blueberry pie. Corina's grandfather *loved* pie.

The second special thing was that it snowed. Corina and the goose caught snowflakes on their tongues. They went sliding on the bluff, and made snow angels (and snow geese) in the front yard.

Corina found the third special thing that evening when she went to the barn to do her chores.

"Look, Granddad!" she cried, pointing to the tiny white lamb curled up beside his mother. "Missy had her baby! I guess Christmas *did* come early this year!"

Corina's grandmother came out to look too.

Finally, when Missy and her new baby had been fussed over and fed and bedded down for the night, Corina and her grandparents walked back up to the house together.

What a sight met their eyes!

The goose had eaten every single one of Gran's Christmas pies.

"GADZOOKS!" roared Granddad...and he grabbed Gran's biggest roasting pan.

Corina grabbed the goose and skedaddled.

Corina and the goose snuggled together in the barn until the sky was full of winking, blinking Christmas stars. Then Corina made a nest for the goose next to Missy and her new baby.

"You silly goose," sighed Corina, pulling the straw up around him. "You'd better sleep out here tonight. Tomorrow is Christmas dinner, so *please* be good or I'm afraid your goose may be cooked!"

Corina kissed the goose goodnight. She closed the rickety barn door and walked slowly back up to the house.

The moon shone on the new-fallen snow.

All was quiet and calm.

Then out of that silent night a dark shape appeared.

Sliding through the shadows on silent paws, it slipped across the marsh, up the bluff, and through the farmyard. Sniffling and snuffling with sharp-toothed jaws, it found the rickety barn door with its loose board near the bottom, still ajar.

Corina and her grandparents were sound asleep when a terrible racket sent them tumbling from their beds.

"Gadzooks!" yelled Granddad. "What in the thunder is going on?" He threw open the window.

From the barn came a howling and growling, a bleating and baa-ing, a hissing and crashing.

"Oh no!" gasped Gran. "Missy's new lamb!"

They dashed to the barn, bathrobes flying. Granddad yanked open the old, crooked door. A large black shape came barrelling out. With a yip and a yowl, it bolted over the bluff and was gone.

Inside the barn, signs of the battle were everywhere.

Straw, feathers, and coyote fur drifted through the air like confetti. In the middle of the floor lay a single tuft of soft, white wool.

"Gad*zooks*," Granddad sighed sadly.

"Oh dear," said Gran, putting her hand over her mouth.

"Goose?" called Corina. "Missy? Baby?"

But all was still.

With a slow, heavy step, Granddad walked to Missy's stall. Lifting the lantern, he peered into the shadows. "GAD*ZOOKS*!" bellowed Granddad, sounding amazed.

For standing in that narrow stall, wings outstretched from wall to wall, was one Very Tough Bird. A tuft of black fur was clenched tight in his beak. Behind him huddled Missy and her lamb, safe and sound.

"Gad*zooks*!" Granddad said again, softly this time. "Bird, I guess you cooked *that* coyote's goose!"

The next morning was Christmas. The goose was invited
inside to help open the presents.

He was very good at it.

There was even a present
just for him.